MY DAD'S A TRADIE
AND SO IS MY MUM

MY DAD'S A TRADIE

and SO IS MY MUM

Missy and Beefy

Illustrations by Shane Ogilvie

About the Authors

Missy is an Australian bull terrier and never misses a day when she can go to work with her dad in his ute.

Beefy is an Australian bulldog who loves going to work with his dad but sometimes he would prefer to stay at home and play with his ball.

Missy and Beefy are at it again on their next adventure to meet and learn about other tradies and see what they do.

Beefy is now 4 years old but Missy knows she still has to babysit her baby brother.

Their dad is a tradie.

Beefy's parents are going on a holiday soon and will fly there in a plane. Beefy wants to learn more about planes so his parents take him to the airport so he can see what a plane looks like.

Beefy sees a hangar and runs inside to see the plane.

"Hello! I'm Beefy. Are you a tradie?"

"Hello Beefy," says a woman working on the aeroplane engine. "Yes, I am a tradie. My name is Alison and I'm an aircraft engineer. I look after aeroplane engines and fix them if they break," she says as she starts up the engines.

"Brrrr! It's windy and noisy," says Beefy.

EXIT
FI
XIT

While Beefy is at the airport he notices a hose with water flowing onto the floor.

Beefy is trying to control the leaking hose when a man comes to help.

"Hello! I'm Beefy. Are you a tradie like my dad?"

"Hi there! Yes I am a tradie. My name is Frankie and I fix fire hydrants. My job is to inspect both the hose and fire hydrant so they are ready to use in a fire emergency."

Beefy happily dances in the puddles. "Yay!" he says, as Frankie tries to fix the hose.

Beefy wants to dry off his paws and wanders into a room that has nice plush carpet.

Then he sees a man wearing strange knee pads.

"Hello, I'm Beefy. Are you a tradie?"

"Sure am! My name is Colin and I'm a carpet layer. I use a special tool called a carpet knee kicker. It sits on top of the carpet and I use my knees to kick it into place."

Then the man makes a loud clacking sound that scares Beefy.

Beefy tries to run away, but trips and gets rolled up in the carpet, becoming a doggie burrito.

Missy is now looking for her brother Beefy as he has wandered off in the airport.

She sees Beefy getting into a lift and jumps in with him. As Beefy starts pressing all the buttons the lift comes to a grinding halt!

"Oh no, we are stuck !" Missy says. "You've done it this time Beefy!"

Luckily a man arrives with tools. "Hello. I'm Beefy and this is Missy. We're stuck! Are you a tradie like our dad?"

"I sure am. My name's Ernie and I'm a lift mechanic! I'll have you out in jiffy," Ernie says, shaking his head.

It's time for Missy and Beefy to head home and Beefy wants to go for a swim at the beach. He sees a man working on a boat in a nearby garage.

"Hello! I'm Beefy. Are you a tradie like my dad?"

"Indeed I am," says the man. "My name is Joel
and I'm a boat builder. I make all types of boats.
This one is a fishing boat and is nearly finished."

Joel gives Beefy a special fishing hat and lifts him into the boat.

"Aye aye captain!" Beefy laughs, as he pretends to be fishing at sea.

The next day, Missy is relieved that they are at home and Beefy can't get into any more trouble, but when Missy and Beefy get up they find a glazier fixing a window.

"Hello, I'm Beefy. Are you a tradie like my dad?"

"Yes, I'm Greg, the glazier. I work with glass. This window has a crack in it so I'm fixing it. When it's finished I'll give it a clean so it looks like new."

"I can help with that," says Beefy, as he holds up a bottle of cleaning spray, but the sprays goes all over the window and the man nearly drops it.

"Thanks Beefy, just don't leave any paw prints!"
laughs Greg.

It's a hot day at home and Beefy and Missy are looking to cool off … but, oh no! The air conditioner is broken!

Luckily a man arrives who can fix it.

"Hello. I'm Beefy and this is Missy. Are you a tradie like our dad?"

"Yes, my name is Aaron and I'm an air-conditioning repairer.
I fix all types of air-conditioning units, in homes or businesses.
This one will be running again in no time at all."

"Great!" says Missy, as they both turn and look at Beefy who is so hot he has nearly melted into the floor!

Beefy and Missy are visiting their baby brother Daniel at school with their mum Nikola when Beefy accidentally locks himself in a classroom. Missy is not impressed. Luckily, a man arrives quickly and begins to work on the door.

"Hello, I'm Missy. Are you a tradie like my dad?"

"Hi Missy, I'm Lewis, and I'm a locksmith. I have small tools that fit inside locks to fix them or to open them when there's no key."

"Phew!" says Missy, shaking her head.

"Piece of cake," Lewis says as he unlocks the door and lets a very relieved Beefy out as his mum shakes her head.

As they leave the school, Beefy and Missy are walking down the road when Beefy trips and lands in a bucket of paint! "Oh nooooo!" says Beefy.

He looks up and sees a lady with a paintbrush.
"Sorry! I'm Beefy. Are you a tradie too?"

"Yes, My name is Yolanda and I'm a sign painter.
I paint pictures and words on walls to advertise a service or a product."

"Well it looks like you'll need some more pink paint now!" says Missy, looking over at Beefy with an angry face.

They all laugh as Beefy washes the paint off.

MILK
YUM

FOR SALE!
SOLD

Further down the road they see a lady putting a sticker on a sign.

"Hello, I'm Beefy. Are you a tradie too?"

"No, I'm not a tradie, I'm Jody. I'm a real estate agent. I sell houses. When someone wants to sell their home or if someone is looking to buy a home, I can help."

"Cowabunga!" says Beefy. "This house looks in need of repair!"

"All good," says Jody, "this one is sold."

"Lucky!" thinks Beefy as he and Missy continue along their way.

Honk! Honk! A big truck pulls around the corner.

"WHOA!" says Beefy, as he climbs up.
"Hi! I'm Beefy. Are you a tradie too?"

"Hiya Beefy, I'm Ray and this is Roxy.
Yes, I'm a tradie and I'm a truckie who drives big trucks collecting and delivering materials with Roxy.
Hop in and let's give you and Missy a ride."

"I'm Roxy and I'm a tradie's dog too!" says Roxy looking out at Beefy.

"Wow," says Beefy. "And you have a loud horn!"

HONK! HONK!

RAY

CITY
CITY

Beefy and Missy continue walking home past the station when they see a train coming.

There is a man waving out the window to them.

"Hello! I'm Beefy and this is Missy. Are you a tradie like our dad?"

"Hello there!" says the man with a big smile. "I'm sort of like a tradie. I'm Tim and I'm a train driver. I make sure the train stops at every station and that all the passengers can board."

Beefy and Missy decide to jump on board and see where the train goes.

Choo, chug and chuff, says the train as it moves away from the station.

Beefy and Missy decide to get off the train and make their way underground, into a mine shaft! They run into a lady pushing a cart on some tracks.

"Hello! I'm Beefy and this is Missy. Are you a tradie too?"

"Yes, I'm Lesley and I'm a miner. I work under the ground digging into rocks to find precious minerals.

"Wow!" say Beefy and Missy at the same time. "What a cool job!"

"It is!" says Lesley. "Now, how about you both jump into my cart and we will go for a ride ...

wheeeeeeeeeeeeeeeeeeeee!!!!!!!!!!!!!!!!"

As Missy and Beefy continue exploring above ground they hear a strange noise. They follow the sound and find themselves in a room with a lot of metal machinery.

"Hello. I'm Beefy and this is Missy. Are you a tradie like our dad?"

"Yes, I'm a tradie. I'm Michael and I'm a fitter and turner. I use my tools to fix metal objects like this water boiler. I have to wear special goggles when using my tools to protect the eyes."

"Like goggles you wear at the beach?" asks Beefy.

"Not quite!" laughs Michael.

Before long Beefy has wandered off again. Missy is looking all over the place for him when she hears a loud bang and a thud.

"Oh no!" says Missy as she sees Beefy has fallen through a stone fireplace.

"Oh noooo!" says Catherine the stonemason.

"Are you a tradie too?" asks Missy, as Catherine helps get Beefy out.

"Yes, I'm a tradie and I work with stone for fireplaces and walls."

"Wow, those stones are heavy," says Missy.

It's time for Beefy and Missy to head home. As they turn into their street they see a huge green truck pull into the park across the road from their house.

Grabbing a spade, they go and see if they can help.

"Hello! I'm Beefy and this is Missy. Are you a tradie too?"

"Absolutely! I'm Lucy and I'm a landscape gardener and a truckie. I plant lots of flowers and trees. And I also deliver the soil for the plants to go into."

"Wow!" says Beefy. "I want to drive a truck too and I want to be a truckie tradie."

Beefy feels like he knows everything about being a tradie now, so he heads to the local construction site with his dad the next day to lend a hand.

"Hi, I'm Beefy, and I know all about being a tradie. Can I help you on your construction site?"

"Hi Beefy, I'm Grant and I'm a project manager. I'd love your help. These are the plans for a building that is being built on this site. What do you think?"

Beefy and Grant look at the plans on the big piece of paper. Beefy feels so proud he is able to help. Everything he has learned from all the tradies he has met on his journey with Missy has paid off.

Beefy is now a tradie too!

First published in 2022 by New Holland Publishers
Sydney

Level 1, 178 Fox Valley Road, Wahroonga, NSW 2076, Australia

newhollandpublishers.com

A record of this book is held at the National Library of Australia.

ISBN 9781760794088

Managing Director: Fiona Schultz
Project Editor: Liz Hardy
Designer: Andrew Davies
Contributor: Catherine Tenisons
Production Director: Arlene Gippert
Printed in China

10 9 8 7 6 5 4 3 2 1

Keep up with New Holland Publishers:

NewHollandPublishers
@newhollandpublishers

Authors:
Missy an Australian bull terrier who loves going to work in her dad's ute and going for boat rides.

Beefy an Australian bulldog who loves playing with his toys and loves balls.

Thank you to Chris Scaife from Coolibah Building & Design.

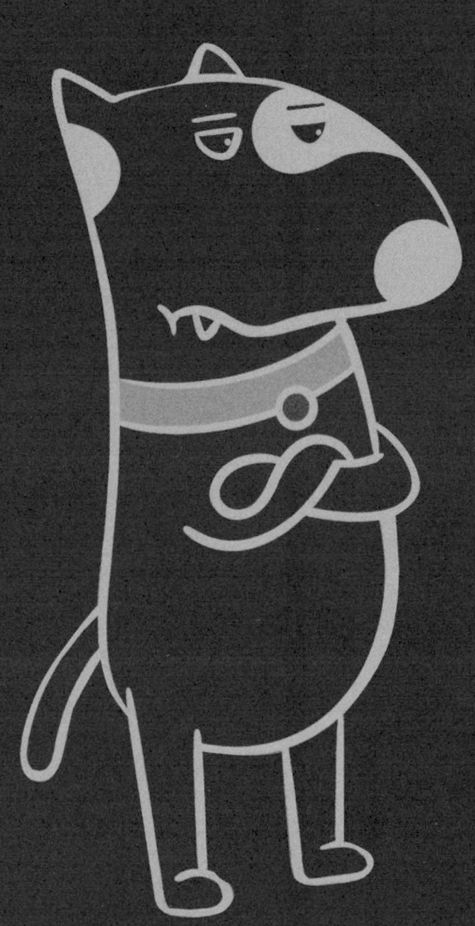